Cinderella

Twin Books

Once upon a time, in a tiny kingdom far away, there lived a widowed gentleman and his beautiful daughter, Cinderella. He was a kind, devoted father who loved his daughter very much, but he felt she needed a mother's care. And so he married a second time, to a widow from a good family. She had two daughters, Anastasia and Drizella, who were close to Cinderella's age.

Soon Cinderella's father met with an untimely, tragic death and his new wife's true nature was revealed.

She became cold, cruel and bitterly jealous of Cinderella's charm and beauty. Completely at the mercy of her step-mother and spiteful stepsisters, Cinderella was forced to become a servant in her own home.

In spite of this misfortune, and of sleeping in the attic with mice and birds for her companions, she remained a gentle, loving girl. Each day as she awoke, fresh from dreaming, she would sing to her friends the bluebirds about her hopes for the future and about the dreams that she wished would one day come true.

Every morning she would finish her song and begin endless chores, sewing, mending, scrubbing, cleaning, waiting on her lazy family hand and foot.

Cinderella didn't know it, but things would soon be different.

It started one morning when Jaq jumped on her dresser, chattering excitedly.

A stranger to the house was caught in a trap at the top of the stairs.

"Why, Jaq, who is this?" asked Cinderella as she set the frightened creature free. Of course, Jaq didn't know, so she said they would call him Octavius—"Gus" for short.

"Hello, Gus. Welcome," she said, and she gave him one of the little caps and shirts she made for her friends.

"Breakfast time! Everybody up!" called Cinderella, throwing fat yellow grains of corn around the barnyard. Bruno the dog awoke from his dream, which was always the same: chasing Lucifer, the mean black cat.

"Come on, everybody—breakfast!" Cinderella called. The animals ran to her from all directions.

"Breakfast? You mean she feeds us?" asked Gus, who was very fond of eating.

"Yes! Come on, everybody! Let's eat," said Jaq.

"Oh, boy! I'm starving!" said Gus, running along with the other mice.

"Wait, be careful," called Jaq. "We have to watch out for the…

…cat!" The big cat sat just outside the mouse hole, toying with his bowl of milk.

Gus shrank back in horror.

"That's Lucifer," said Jaq. "But I know how to get around him. I will be the decoy, and when I signal, you men run up behind him. Got it?"

So Jaq ran bravely across the kitchen, so close to the cat's nose he could feel his whiskers, and dived for a mouse hole in the baseboard just ahead of Lucifer's sharp claws.

The others dashed behind them and ran out to the barnyard.

Now, one plump golden grain of corn is an armload to the average mouse, and two is the most a mouse should carry. But Gus didn't know his limits.

So while Cinderella rushed about tending to the requests and demands of her stepmother and sisters, who were now awake and yelling, Gus loaded himself with more kernels than he could carry.

21

"I'll bet no mouse has ever carried five kernels of corn before," thought Gus, as he smugly imagined how impressed the other mice would be. He was so proud of himself that he didn't hear Jaq warn him about the cat.

Lucifer turned and silently crept up behind him.

When Gus saw the cat, he dropped the corn and ran for his life. He climbed up the cloth to the top of the table and hid in a teacup. But the crafty cat sneaked up behind him and covered the cup with a saucer. Gus was trapped!

Suddenly, the kitchen call bells started ringing.

"Cinderella!" called Anastasia.

"Where is that lazy girl?" cried Drizella. "And where is my breakfast? Cinderella!"

Cinderella dashed inside to make their breakfast. Without looking in the cup, she placed it on the tray—with Gus inside. There was nothing the cat could do.

"Cinderella!" both the frenzied sisters called.

"I'm coming! Just a minute!," said Cinderella, rushing up the stairs.

Even though Lucifer circled her feet and sneaked a peek in one of the teacups, he couldn't catch Gus.

Once again, the mice were safe and Cinderella went upstairs.

"Oh, well," she said to herself, "They can't order me to stop dreaming! Perhaps someday the dream that I wish *will* come true."

A short distance away, in the royal palace, the King was fretting. "My son has been avoiding responsibility long enough! It's high time he married and settled down."

"Yes, Sire," the Duke replied, "but we must be patient."

"I am patient," said the King. "But I'm not getting any younger. I want to see grandchildren before I go.

"I have it," said the King. "We'll throw a ball and invite all the eligible maidens in the kingdom. He's bound to show an interest in one of them, isn't he?"

"Perhaps, Sire…"

"See that *every* eligible maid is there. Immediately!"

And so, that very day, the King sent his messenger to call on every household in the kingdom.

"Open in the name of the King," the messenger called, delivering an invitation to Cinderella's house.

"What is it?" asked Cinderella.

"In honor of His Highness, the Crown Prince, by royal command, every eligible maiden is to attend a Royal Ball!"

"A Royal Ball?" asked Cinderella.

"Every eligible maiden? Why, that's *us*!" cried Anastasia and Drizella.

"Yes," said their scheming mother. "The King has long wanted his son to marry. It must be to one of you. Hurry, girls, the ball is tonight!"

"Why, that means I can go, too," said Cinderella.

"Ha! Her, dancing with the Prince?" said her stepsisters, laughing cruelly.

"It says 'every eligible maiden,'" said Cinderella.

"Well, I see no reason why you can't go…" began her stepmother.

"No, Mother! Don't let her," cried the stepsisters.

"…if you finish all your work and find something suitable to wear," she finished coldly.

Cinderella was elated. She dashed to the attic, threw open a trunk, and pulled out a dress.

"Isn't it lovely? It was my mother's," she said. "Of course, it is a bit old-fashioned. I'll have to fix it up. I'll need a sash, a ruffle, something for the collar…"

"Oh, Cinderella!" called her stepmother.

"Before you begin your regular chores, I have a few little things for you to do…" her stepmother said to Cinderella.

"Yes! Press my skirt," said Drizella.

"Take my dress. Mend the buttonholes," said Anastasia.

And that afternoon, when Cinderella finally had a chance to do her regular chores, even Lucifer wickedly forced her to clean the floor again.

Poor Cinderella! She would never have a chance to touch her dress.

"Poor Cinderelly," said the mice, sadly.

"Work, work, work," said Gus.

"They're doing this on purpose so she won't have a chance to get her dress done," said Jaq.

But suddenly, the mice had an idea. "We can do it! We can help our Cinderelly!" they chimed. "We can make her dress so pretty! We'll add a sash, and ribbons, and a flounce! She'll be the most beautiful girl at the ball!"

The mice sang as they transformed the old dress into a ball gown.

Gus said, "I can cut it with the scissors."

Jaq said, "I'll do the sewing."

But the girl mice said, "Leave the sewing to us women. You two go and get some trimming."

The birds helped, too, and the dress began to take shape.

Under the very nose of the cat, Gus and Jaq collected all the beads of Drizella's discarded necklace and a sash and roll of ribbon thrown in the trash by Anastasia.

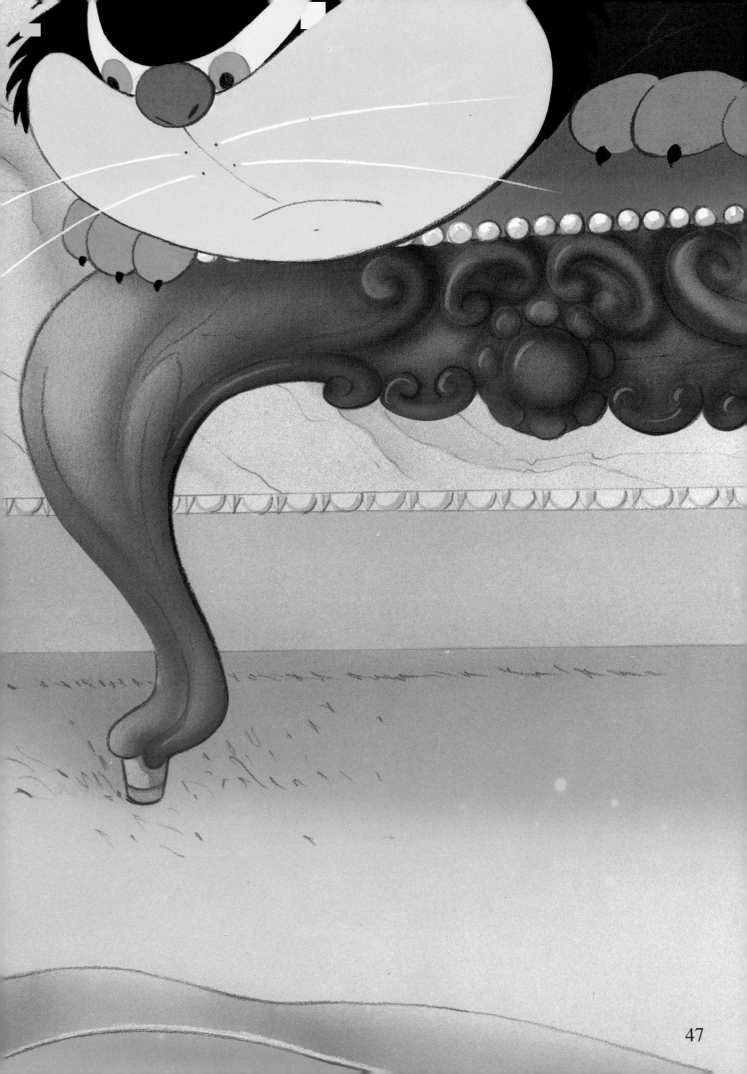

After finishing all her work, Cinderella sadly watched the carriage arrive to take her stepmother and stepsisters to the ball.

"Oh, well," she sighed. "What's a Royal Ball? Dull, boring and…completely *wonderful*!"

Suddenly, the room behind her lit up and she saw the dress, more beautiful than she had imagined it could be, with Drizella's beads and Anastasia's sash and ribbons.

"Surprise!" cried the mice and birds.

"Uh, Happy Birthday," said Gus.

"We fixed it for you, Cinderelly," said Jaq.

Cinderella could hardly believe her eyes.

"Why, I never dreamed…what a surprise! How can I ever, ever thank you? Oh, thank you so much!" cried Cinderella.

She quickly put on the beautiful dress and dashed down to catch the carriage.

But the jealous stepsisters recognized the things they had thrown away.

"Look, that's my sash!" cried Anastasia, snatching it away.

"Why, you little thief, they're my beads!" shrieked Drizella, pulling at them.

"My ribbon! Give it back!"

When they were finished snatching and grabbing and pulling at Cinderella's dress, it was in tatters. Then the stepsisters and their mother smugly set off for the ball.

Cinderella ran outside, past
the horse and dog and into the
garden, sobbing. Gus, Jaq, and
two other mice had followed
her, and stood by silently.

Buried in her tears,
Cinderella didn't see a magic
light swirl and grow bigger and
slowly take form.

"There's nothing left to believe in, nothing!" sobbed Cinderella.

"Nothing, my dear?" asked a voice. "Now you don't really mean that."

Startled, Cinderella looked up and saw a kind old lady in a blue robe. "Who are you?" she asked.

"Your fairy godmother, of course," replied the lady. "And I couldn't be here if you'd lost *all* your faith. Now, dry those tears. You can't go to the ball looking like that!"

"The ball? But I'm not going."

"Of course you are! But we'll have to hurry, because even miracles take a little time."

"Miracles?" asked Cinderella.

"Of course. Now fetch me a pumpkin!"

Cinderella did as she was told. Her fairy godmother waved her magic wand and began to sing some magic words.

The pumpkin began to transform into a carriage, right before Cinderella's astonished eyes.

Then the fairy godmother said, "With an elegant coach like that, you simply have to have…*mice!*"

With that, she waved her magic wand over the four mice and magically transformed them into prancing horses.

With another wave of the wand, the old horse and Bruno, the dog, were changed into a coachman and a footman.

"Oh, it's wonderful!" exclaimed Cinderella.

"Well, hop in, my dear. We can't waste time."

"But...um..." mumbled Cinderella.

"Oh, now, don't try to thank me."

"Oh, I wasn't. I mean, I do, but...my dress!"

"Good heavens, child," said her fairy godmother. "You can't go to the ball in that!"

With another wave of the wand, Cinderella was dressed in a beautiful ball gown, wearing a gleaming pair of glass slippers.

"Oh, it's so beautiful!" cried Cinderella. "Why, it's like a dream come true!"

"And like all dreams, this one can't last forever," said her fairy godmother. "At midnight, when the clock strikes twelve, the spell will be broken and everything will be as it was before."

"Oh, I'll remember," said Cinderella.

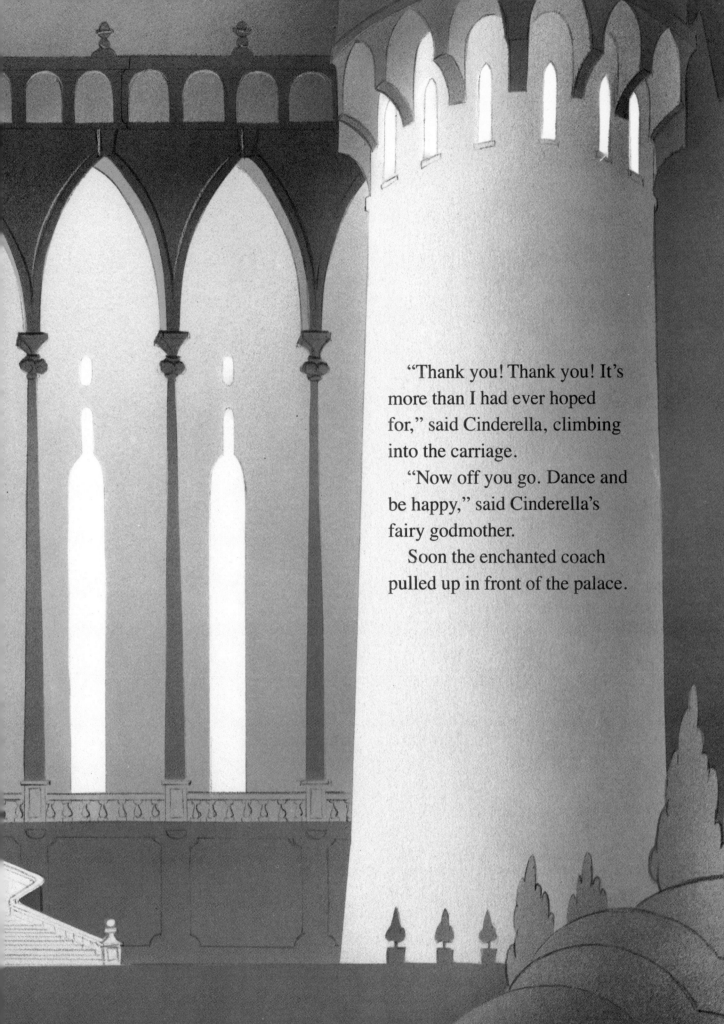

"Thank you! Thank you! It's more than I had ever hoped for," said Cinderella, climbing into the carriage.

"Now off you go. Dance and be happy," said Cinderella's fairy godmother.

Soon the enchanted coach pulled up in front of the palace.

With an excited heart and more joy than she had ever known, Cinderella ascended the palatial staircase. She heard them announcing other people's names, Princess Frederica Eugenie, and M'amselle Augustina Dubois....

In the balcony, the King and the Duke watched Cinderella enter. They also saw the Prince, bored to distraction, take notice for the first time all evening.

"Do you know her?" asked the King.

"I've never seen her before," said the Grand Duke.

"Look, he's walking toward her," cried the King. "Quickly! Turn down the lights. Start the waltz!"

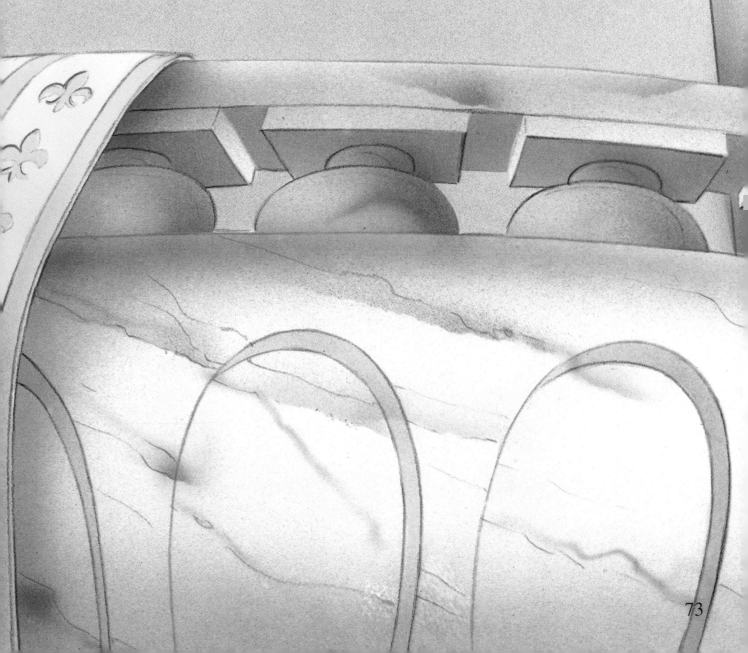

The handsome Prince swept past all the other maidens and took Cinderella in his arms just as the waltz began. They danced with eyes only for each other, as if no one else existed in the world.

Cinderella had found the love she'd been dreaming about. She was so happy with the Prince that the evening passed quickly.

When they were alone, in the starlight, the Prince leaned down to kiss her. But the clock suddenly began its ominous chime: one…two…three…

"It's midnight," gasped Cinderella. "I must go!"

"Oh, no! Wait! You can't go now," cried the Prince.

"I must," she said, and she dashed away.

The awful clock kept chiming: four…five…six…

Cinderella ran out of the palace so quickly she lost one of her glass slippers. It was left lying on the stair.

With the Prince and the Duke and all the palace guards in hot pursuit. Cinderella leaped inside her carriage and raced away.

The clock kept striking: seven… eight… nine… ten… eleven…

At the stroke of twelve, the running horses changed into running mice. There was Cinderella, dressed in rags, sitting on a pumpkin.

"I'm sorry," Cinderella said to her little friends. "I forgot about everything, even the time. But it was so wonderful! And he was so handsome! And when we danced…."

Jaq chattered and pointed to Cinderella's feet.

"What?" asked Cinderella.

Then she saw that she still had one glass slipper.

The King had fallen asleep while the Prince was dancing. He was still dreaming of a chubby grandson when the exhausted Duke woke him up to tell him that Cinderella had disappeared.

"What? You must find her!" cried the King.

And so, while Cinderella danced about the kitchen humming the waltz she had danced in the arms of the Prince, her stepmother watched suspiciously and the King sent the Duke to scour the Kingdom for the maiden whose foot would fit his only clue—the glass slipper.

Knowing that the girl who fit the slipper would be the Prince's bride, the wicked stepmother locked Cinderella in her room.

While Anastasia did everything she could to get more than her toe into the tiny slipper, Jaq and Gus got the key to Cinderella's door out of the stepmother's pocket, and began to push it up the stairs.

They were almost thwarted by the cat, who sat on the top stair with an evil glint in his eye. But luckily, Bruno heard their cries and chased Lucifer away.

Cinderella, free at last, dashed down the stairs.
"Please, may I try the slipper on?" she asked.
But her crafty stepmother tripped the footman. The slipper
fell to the floor and shattered.

"Oh, no! What will the King do?" cried the Duke in dismay.

Cinderella sat in the chair and reached into her pocket.

"Perhaps this would help…" she said.

"No, nothing will help!" cried the the Duke.

"But, you see, I have the other slipper," said Cinderella. Her stepsisters gasped, but the Duke was overjoyed. He fitted the slipper on Cinderella's foot.

"Perfect!" he cried. "We have found the Prince's bride!"

And so Cinderella and the Prince were married. The King watched fondly, thinking of the grandchildren who would sit on his knee. The Grand Duke smiled, too, because the King would be happy at last.

Cinderella and her Prince smiled because they had found each other.

And Cinderella's friends the mice smiled and waved because they knew their lovely "Cinderelly" would be the happiest woman in the kingdom.

Produced by
Twin Books
15 Sherwood Place
Greenwich, CT. 06830,
USA

ISBN 1-85469-972-5

Printed in Hong Kong

1 2 3 4 5 6 7 8 9 10

The prince and a radiantly
happy Cinderella were
married. They lived happily
ever after and the old king
had many grand-children.